SUPER SHORTS

Awesome Animal Stories

KINGFISHER
a Houghton Mifflin Company imprint
222 Berkeley Street
Boston, Massachusetts 02116
www.houghtonmifflinbooks.com

First published in 2007
2 4 6 8 10 9 7 5 3 1

LIBRARY OF CONGRESS CATALOGING-IN-PUBLICATION DATA
has been applied for.

ISBN 978-0-7534-6071-9

Printed in China
1TR/0707/PROSP/MAR/80NEWSP/C

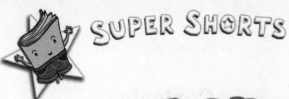

SUPER SHORTS

Awesome Animal Stories

compiled by Elizabeth Holland

KINGFISHER

BOSTON

Contents

Crocodile Tears

Joyce Dunbar

Two mother crocodiles were basking by the river, their jaws wide open in the sun.

They were very proud crocodiles because their eggs had successfully hatched, and in each of their mouths was a tiny baby crocodile.

But these mother crocodiles had a problem. It was time for their babies to leave the comfortable pouch in their jaws and join the other baby crocodiles in the swamp, but the babies just wouldn't let go. They were frightened of the big, wide world.

The mother crocodiles looked at each other, chewing over their problem. This in itself wasn't easy, for it is very hard to chew anything at all when you have a lot of sharp teeth and a small baby crocodile in your mouth.

"I've never known a baby to

be so clingy," said the first mother
crocodile. "He wants me to carry him
everywhere."

"Mine's just the same," said the
second mother crocodile. "I've coaxed
and cajoled, but this baby will not be
put down. I have to eat on one side of
my mouth. Just try that when you're
attempting to dig into a wart hog."

"I know how it is," said the first mother crocodile. "So tiresome."

Then, with their jaws still wide open in the sun, cozily cradling their babies, the mother crocodiles went to sleep.

A crocodile bird came along, pick-pick-picking at the teeth of the first mother crocodile for pieces of food left between the teeth. Her baby didn't like this. They were *his* pieces of food. He gave a snap with his baby jaws, but the crocodile bird escaped. It flew to the second mother crocodile's

jaws. Pick-pick-pick, it went again.

The second mother's baby also gave a sharp snap with his baby jaws. Again the crocodile bird escaped.

"Yah! Missed!" said the first baby crocodile to the second baby crocodile.

"So did you!" said the second baby crocodile, peeping between his mother's teeth.

"So what if I did?" said the first baby crocodile. "My mom's bigger than yours."

"So what if she is bigger?" said the second baby crocodile. "My mom's scalier than yours."

"So what if she is scalier?" said the

first baby crocodile. "My mom can swim faster than yours. She catches more fish."

"Well, my mom caught a shark this morning," said the second baby crocodile. "And she ate it all, and that was just for breakfast."

"I don't believe you," said the first baby crocodile. "There aren't any sharks around here. Anyway, my mom frightened some people this morning. Three people in a boat. She frightened them away."

"Did she *only* frighten them?" said the first baby crocodile. "My mom catches people. She catches them and puts them in the fridge."

"No, she doesn't," said the second baby crocodile. "Because my mom went looking in your mom's fridge yesterday, and there weren't any people there. There was only a skinny water rat."

"Oh, did your mom go looking in my mom's fridge?" said the first baby crocodile. "Well, I'll tell my mom when she wakes up. My mom will take a bite

out of your mom."

"Oh, will she?" said the second baby crocodile. "I'd like to see her try. My mom has a lot more teeth than your mom."

"How do you know that?" asked the first crocodile. "You can't count!"

"Oh, yes, I can!" said the second baby crocodile. "Three. One hundred. Seventy-one. Four thousand."

"Well, my

mom's teeth are sharper and longer than your mom's teeth, so there!"

"How do you know that?" asked the second baby crocodile. "You can't measure!"

"Just you come along here and take a look!" said the first baby crocodile.

"I will an' all," said the second baby crocodile, "and you just come along here and take a look."

"I will an' all," said the first baby crocodile. By this time, the two baby crocodiles had forgotten all about how frightened they were of the big, wide world. The first baby crocodile slithered out of his mother's jaws and started to make his way to the jaws of the second mother crocodile.

The second baby crocodile slithered out of his mother's jaws and started to make his way to the jaws of the first mother crocodile.

They passed each other on the way.

"Hey, look!" said the first baby crocodile. "We're down on the ground!"

"So we are!" said the second baby crocodile. "On our own four legs!"

They swished their tails and snapped

their jaws happily at each other.

"There's the swamp," said the first baby crocodile, "and a whole lot more baby crocodiles. Why don't we go for a splash?"

"We can count teeth later," said the second baby crocodile, belly crawling along after him.

The crocodile bird saw his chance. Pick-pick-pick, he went on the first mother's teeth and then pick-pick-pick on the other.

Suddenly, the mothers woke up.

"Where's my baby?" said the first mother crocodile.

"Where's mine?" said the second mother crocodile.

They raced down to the edge of the swamp. There they found the two baby crocodiles, playing and splashing with all of the other baby crocodiles.

"Ah! Aren't they sweet?" they said to each other, grinning from eye to eye.

Then they wept great big crocodile tears.

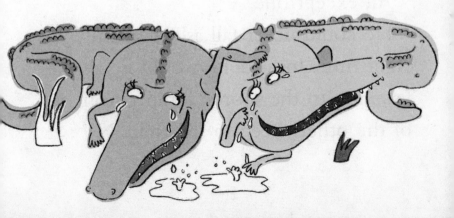

The Lamb Who Couldn't Sleep

John Yeoman

It was springtime in the marshes, and every day the young lambs raced around the fields and jumped and turned in the air. Every evening, they settled down beside their mothers, out of the wind, and fell fast asleep.

All except one.

He could never fall asleep at the right time. Instead, he would lie awake listening to the snores coming from all of the other sheep in the field. No

matter how hard he tried, he just didn't
seem to be able to fall asleep. What was
worse, just as the first faint light of the
sun began to appear over the hedge
and the mist began to clear from the
field, he would start to doze off.

Every morning began the same way.

"Time to get up," said his mother.
"It's going to be a lovely morning.
Have a little drink and nibble
some fresh grass,
and then

you can go off and play with your friends."

Through his sleepy, half-opened eyes, the lamb could see some of his friends already leaping and spinning around the field.

"I don't think I want to play yet," he said and gave a big yawn.

"Oh, dear," said his mother. "Didn't you sleep very well?"

"No," he said. "I didn't sleep at all. I never do."

"Why don't you try counting sheep tonight?" his mother suggested.

That night he took his mother's advice. As he snuggled down beside her, sheltered from the breeze, he began to count. Because he was a very young lamb, he could only count up to three, but he thought that counting up to three over and over again was probably as good as counting up to 100 once.

"One, two, THREE . . . one, two, THREE . . . one, two, THREE . . . one, two, THREE."

"What does that young fool think he's doing?" came the voice of a sheep out of the darkness.

"Sounds like he's starting a race," came a reply.

"Is he trying to get us to join in a song?" suggested another.

"I think you're keeping the others

awake," his mother
whispered. "That's
enough counting for
tonight." The lamb
just sighed, rested his
chin on his front feet,
and settled down for
another sleepless night.

After breakfast the next morning, he
staggered across the field to say hello
to his friends. But his eyes were so
bleary and his legs were so unsteady
that he stumbled right into a big
oak tree.

"It isn't good
manners to go

bumping into people's homes like that," said a voice from above.

The lamb looked up and saw an owl sitting on a branch.

"I'm very sorry," said the lamb. "I'm so tired that I didn't see the tree."

"How can you be tired?" snapped the owl. "You haven't done anything yet!"

"I didn't sleep. I never do."

"Deary me," said the owl in a softer voice. "We will have

to do something about that. Come back to see me this afternoon, and I'll give you some of my special sleeping mixture."

"Oh, thank you," said the lamb.

And he set off to join his friends, feeling much better already.

Back at the oak tree after lunch, he was a little disappointed to find that the owl hadn't been able to make his special sleeping mixture.

"It's almost ready," the bird explained, "but I'm afraid I'm short of one or two items. Would you be kind enough to bring me a feather that has dropped from a crow, please? That fellow there has a loose one sticking out, do you see?"

The lamb raced after the crow, which waited until he was close by before flying up and landing a few feet away.

The lamb gave chase again, and the crow did exactly

the same thing. It happened again and again, until finally the feather came free and fluttered to the ground.

As quick as a flash, the lamb picked it up in his mouth and ran back to the tree.

"Well done," said the owl. "Just leave it there while you go to look for the other thing."

"You mean there's more?" panted the lamb.

"Well, you want the mixture to work properly, don't you?" asked the owl. Yes, the lamb certainly wanted the mixture to work properly.

"Good," said the owl. "Now, you see that black lamb over there? He's got a

particular kind of
thistle sticking
to his fleece.
Just bring me
that, and then
we'll be ready."
The lamb
bounded off
again. When the
black lamb saw him
coming, he thought
that it was a game and
raced away as fast as he could. They
ran and ran, this way and that way,
across the field, for ages and ages—
until finally the thistle dropped off
and the lamb was able to pick it up.

He returned to the tree, all hot and puffed out.

"That's exactly what we need," said the owl. "Unfortunately, it's too late this afternoon to finish making the mixture. But you will have it tomorrow. Go back to your mother now."

It was getting dark when the lamb got back to his mother.

"Had a nice afternoon?" she asked.

And do you know—he was so worn out that he just lay down and fell asleep.

The next morning he was completely refreshed from his good night's sleep

and couldn't wait to tell the owl.

"I slept soundly all night!" he said.

"I thought you might," said the owl with a wink. "So you won't be needing my mixture after all. You see, it's my belief that you'll sleep well every night from now on."

And the wise old owl was right. The lamb spent every day running around

with his friends, and every night he fell asleep as soon as he closed his eyes.

And I hope you do too.

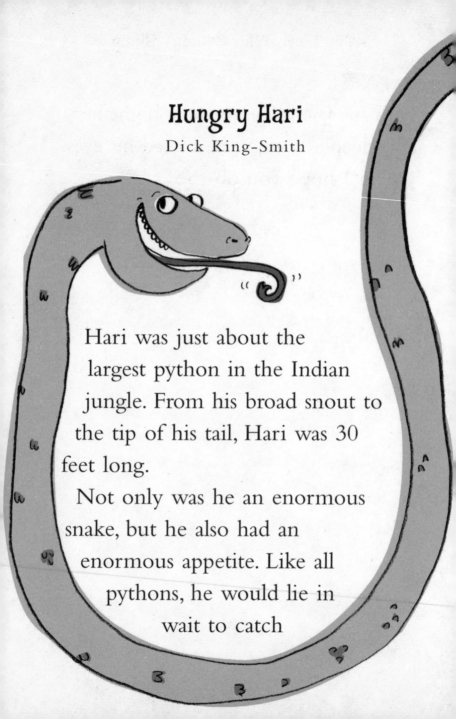

Hungry Hari

Dick King-Smith

Hari was just about the
largest python in the Indian
jungle. From his broad snout to
the tip of his tail, Hari was 30
feet long.

Not only was he an enormous
snake, but he also had an
enormous appetite. Like all
pythons, he would lie in
wait to catch

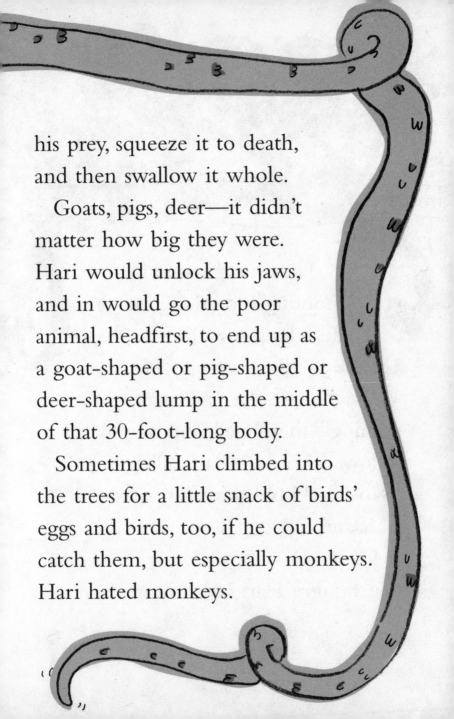

his prey, squeeze it to death,
and then swallow it whole.

Goats, pigs, deer—it didn't
matter how big they were.
Hari would unlock his jaws,
and in would go the poor
animal, headfirst, to end up as
a goat-shaped or pig-shaped or
deer-shaped lump in the middle
of that 30-foot-long body.

Sometimes Hari climbed into
the trees for a little snack of birds'
eggs and birds, too, if he could
catch them, but especially monkeys.
Hari hated monkeys.

They hung around,
shouting rude things at him
and telling the other animals
of the jungle where he was.

"Watch out, the giant worm is
coming!" they cried, and they
followed Hari around, calling him
"No Legs!" and throwing nuts and
fruit and twigs at him.

There was one particular monkey
that hungry Hari hated more than

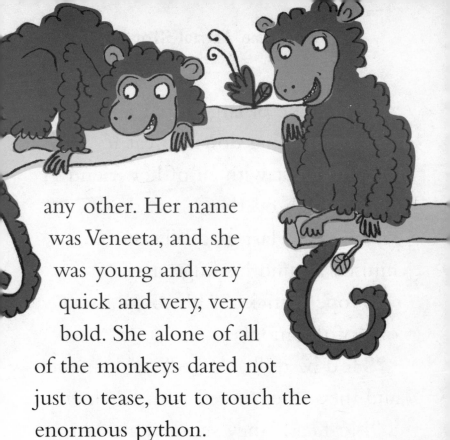

any other. Her name
was Veneeta, and she
was young and very
quick and very, very
bold. She alone of all
of the monkeys dared not
just to tease, but to touch the
enormous python.

It happened one sultry afternoon
when the jungle creatures were
sheltering from the burning sun and
dozing in the shade of the giant trees.
Hari had just caught and killed a young

nilgai, a type of large forest antelope, and was settling down to eat it.

Veneeta sat with all of her friends on a branch overhead, and they watched as Hari gradually moved himself around his huge meal.

"Hope it sticks in his throat," said one of the monkeys.

"He'd be really choked!" said another, and they all chattered with laughter.

"No Legs!" they shouted at Hari and "No Brains!" and they danced around on the branch and made faces.

All the time the nilgai moved slowly along inside Hari, until at last it stopped, a nilgai-shaped lump right in the middle of his 30-foot-long body.

"Now," said Veneeta, "watch me, all of you."

"What are you going to do?" asked the others.

"Pull his tail," said Veneeta.

"You wouldn't dare!" they said.

"Wait and see," she said, and she ran down the tree, as quick as a flash, grabbed ahold of the tip of Hari's tail, and gave it a tweak.

The news spread around the jungle like wildfire. Veneeta the monkey had dared to tweak hungry Hari's tail!

The peacocks, whose call is very loud, flew up into the treetops and cried the tidings so that everyone knew, from the smallest forest shrew to the mighty tiger.

And now, wherever Hari went, all of the creatures of the jungle would mock him, telling him that he needed eyes in the back of his head.

"Watch out for Veneeta!" they cried. "She can't pull your leg, but she'll pull your tail again if you don't watch out!"

And she did. Each time she would wait until Hari had eaten a long meal and there was a something-shaped lump in the middle of that long, long body. And then, knowing how sluggish he would be with a full belly, Veneeta would dart down and grab the tip of his tail.

At first she only pulled it, but one day, growing even more daring, she actually gave it a nip, sinking her sharp little teeth into the extreme end of hungry Hari before darting away while all of her friends cheered and jeered.

Once again the peacocks cried the amazing news. Veneeta the

monkey had dared to bite hungry
Hari's tail! What next? Would she
dance upon his body perhaps, this
sassy Veneeta? Would she run along its
30-foot length and bite him on the
nose and be gone before the giant
worm could catch her?

To catch Veneeta became the most
important thing in Hari's life. Every
night now he slithered among the
branches of the great trees, looking
for her. Many a monkey went

headfirst down that endless throat,
but never the one he wanted, the
one he hated, the one that had
had the impudence to bite the
tip of his tail.

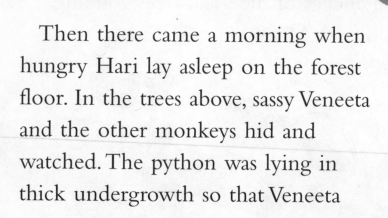

Then there came a morning when
hungry Hari lay asleep on the forest
floor. In the trees above, sassy Veneeta
and the other monkeys hid and
watched. The python was lying in
thick undergrowth so that Veneeta

could see only his big, blunt head at
one end and his tail tip at the other.
What shape of lump there might be
in the middle she could not see.

In fact, there was no lump, for Hari

had had a poor night's hunting,
catching only a single monkey, whose
body was too small to alter his shape.

Should I risk it? Veneeta thought.
That tail tip was so tempting. She
jumped down, but as she jumped,

Hari stirred. Some instinct told him that his hated tormentor was near.

He looked around, still half asleep, and he stretched, flexing the million muscles in his long, long body, from his head to the end of his tail, which twitched.

Veneeta saw the movement of the tail tip, and so did Hari. With lightning speed, he struck.

"Look!" cried Veneeta to all of her friends. "The python is eating himself!"

So hungry was Hari that at first he did not realize what he was doing. So wide open were his jaws that he could not see what it was that he was swallowing.

That monkey's taking a long time to go down, he said to himself, *and what's more, my tail feels as though something's eating it.*

Then suddenly he saw Veneeta dancing around him, while up above her friends cheered and jeered. Only then, when two or three of his 30 feet

were inside him, did hungry Hari understand what was happening.

By now the peacocks had spread the news throughout the jungle, and all of the creatures, from the smallest forest shrew to the mighty tiger, came to watch the amazing sight of hungry Hari the python devouring himself.

Everyone watched intently, except Veneeta, who was now so excited that she did not notice that Hari had stopped swallowing his tail and was beginning to pull it back out again.

"Look at old No Legs!" she cried to them all, turning her back on the python. "Look at old No Brains! You know the trouble with him, don't you? He's too full of himself!"

Then suddenly everyone saw the danger that the sassy monkey was in and called out to warn her.

"Veneeta, Veneeta!" they all cried, which sounded to Hari, who was almost deaf, like "Eat her! Eat her!"

In the nick of time, Veneeta leaped into the air as the python's big, blunt head whizzed underneath her.

"Misssssed," said hungry Hari softly as Veneeta and her friends swung away through the trees. "But I'll sssssswallow you one day, sssssee if I don't."

He never did, though.

For while sassy Veneeta still shouted rude things at hungry Hari whenever

she saw him, there was one thing that
she never dared to touch again.

You know what it was, don't you?
The end of that tail.
(And that's the end of this tale.)

Hot Hippos

Sally Grindley

It was hot. Very, very hot. The lions were hot, the giraffes were hot, the zebras were hot. But hottest of all were the hippos. And a hot hippo is not a happy hippo.

"When is it going to rain?" grumbled Harriet. "All of this sun is making my skin feel like an elephant's behind."

"I don't think it's ever going to rain again," moaned Henry. "Soon the last drop of water in the lake will have dried up, and then where will we be?" The lake was now so small that only one hippo could fit in it at a time. The hippos had made a list and were taking turns to go for a wallow. Hepzibah was the lucky hippo wallowing now while the others sweltered.

"Soon it'll be my turn," said Harriet. "Five more minutes, Hepzi."

"Well, don't splash this time," said Hepzibah. "You wasted a lot of water bouncing around last time."

"I'm not waiting for my next turn," said Henry. "I'm off. I don't want to look like a shriveled prune."

Hepzibah and Harriet looked at him in astonishment.

"You're going?" said Harriet. "But where? We've always lived here. How will you find another lake? You might get lost."

"Better than staying here," said Henry. "That puddle will be gone by tomorrow, and there's hardly any grass left to eat."

Harriet frowned and shed a hot, salty tear that instantly dried on her hot hippo skin. She looked at

Hepzibah. Even though she had bunched herself up to make herself as small as possible, there was no room in the water for her behind. Only her feet and ample belly were submerged. She had to accept that their once magnificent lake was now no more

than a pitiful puddle. But it was still all the water they had, and she was terrified at the thought of leaving it. Then Hepzibah heaved her hefty bulk out of the water and said, "You're right, Henry. No point in staying here to wallow in self-pity—and that's all there will be to wallow in. I'm coming too."

"What about you, Harriet?" said Henry. "You can't stay here on your own. As soon as the sun goes down and it's cooler, we'll set off."

Late that evening, the three hippos each took one final lingering roll in the shrinking puddle, tore at the last few threads of

brown grass, and began their long,
slow journey in search of water and
food. They walked at night, munched
on any pieces of greenery that they
could find in the evening and early
morning, and sat under trees and
dozed when the midday sun made
it too hot to do anything.

Four days passed,
and the hippos were
growing weaker
and weaker. They
ached all over
from so much
walking, their
bellies rumbled
with hunger, their

feet were sore and blistered, and their dry, cracked skin hung loosely from them as they grew thinner and thinner. They began to give up hope that they would ever find water again, when one evening Henry suddenly stopped and pointed.

"Look, what's that? Over there. Behind those trees. There's something shiny. Stay here while I go and see."

He bounded through the undergrowth as fast as a tired, hot, and hungry hippo could go, and when he reached the other side of the trees, he stopped and shouted back, "It's water! Come and see—it's water!"

And with that, he leaped into the

water
and rolled
and splashed and
kicked and gurgled
and behaved just like a
small child in a swimming pool.
Hepzibah and Harriet weren't far
behind, and when they reached the
water, they jumped in with loud
squeals of delight. Just at that moment
it would have been difficult to find
three happier hippos anywhere.

That night they went to sleep under
the trees, and in the early morning
they explored their new home. The

lake wasn't as big as their old one, but there were two more next to it, and all around there was lush green grass and beautiful trees and bushes. When the day began to warm up, they sat in the lake and thought how good life was. Then they spotted something that they had never seen before. It was like rain, but it was coming from one spot, and it was going up into the air and

around and around.

Hepzibah couldn't contain herself. She leaped from the lake, bounded across the grass, and danced around under the spray in a strange sort of hippo rumba.

That's when it happened. Something hard hit Harriet on her snout.

"Ouch!" she cried. "That hurt. Who's throwing things?"

Then the same thing happened to Henry. "Hey!" he cried. "Someone's throwing things." And he picked up what looked like a round, white stone out of the water.

The two hippos looked around them and suddenly saw two people walking toward the lake carrying metal sticks in their hands and long bags over their backs.

"This looks like trouble," said Henry. "Duck!"

Harriet and Henry both ducked quickly, but Hepzibah was blissfully unaware that she was about to be spotted.

"Hey, what's that under the sprinkler?" a first voice cried.

"Well, bless my soul," exclaimed the other voice. "That looks like a hippo to me. And look, there's another one and another one. How on earth did they get there?"

The two men ran off to tell the

world, leaving the hippos to wonder
what would happen.

Before very long, crowds of people
lined the golf course, trying to catch
a glimpse of the hippos. Huge cheers
went up every time that Henry,

Harriet, and Hepzibah raised their heads from the lake. Some of the golfers got angry because so many people were wandering over the green that they couldn't continue with their games, and they had to miss three of the holes because they were scared to get too close to the hippos.

The golfers wanted to have the hippos taken away, but everyone else was so angry at the suggestion that the golfers were forced to leave them where they were. A special enclosure was built around the hippos' lake to protect them, and the golfers just had to put up with a slight alteration to their course and one fewer lake.

As for the hippos, they had water, and they had grass, and they soon learned that if a golfer shouted the warning "FORE," they should duck right under the water to avoid a painful blow to the head.

The Magpie's Nest

Michael Rosen

Once, a long time ago, when the winter was almost over and the spring had almost begun, all of the birds were busy starting to build their nests. There they all were—the robin, the eagle, the seagull, the blackbird, the duck, the owl, and the hummingbird—all busy. All, that is, except Magpie. And she didn't feel much like working.

It was a nice day, and she was out and about looking for scrips and scraps and bits and pieces for her collection of old junk—her hoard of bits and pieces that she had picked up from behind chimneys or from drainpipes. Pebbles, beads, buttons, and the like—anything bright and interesting or unusual—Magpie was sure to collect. Just as she was flying along on the lookout for a new treasure, she caught sight of Sparrow, her mouth full of pieces of straw and twigs.

"What are you doing, what are you doing?" asked Magpie.

"Building my nest," said Sparrow, "like you'll have to do soon."

"Oh, yes?" said Magpie.

"Yes," said Sparrow, "put that milk-
bottle cap down and come over here
and watch. First you have to find a
twig and then another twig, another
twig, another twig, another twig . . ."

"Don't make me laugh," said
Magpie, "I know, I know, I know all
that," and off she flew. And as she
flew on looking for scrips and scraps
and bits and pieces she came to Duck,
who was upside down with her
mouth full of mud.

"What are you doing, what are you

doing?" asked Magpie.

"Building my nest," said Duck, "like you'll have to do soon."

"Oh, yes?" said Magpie.

"Yes," said Duck, "throw away that old earwig and watch me. After you've got all of your twigs, you have to stick them with mud pats like this—pat-pat, pat-pat, pat-pat . . ."

"Don't make me laugh," said Magpie, "I know, I know, I know all

that," and off she flew. And as she flew on looking for scrips and scraps and bits and pieces she saw Pigeon with a mouthful of feathers.

"What are you doing, what are you doing?" asked Magpie.

"Building my nest," said Pigeon, "like you'll have to do soon."

"Oh, yes?" said Magpie.

"Yes," said Pigeon, "put that bus ticket down and come over here and learn how. You have to make yourself warm and cozy—okay? Okay. So you dig your beak into your chest like this—okay? And find one of those very soft, fluffy feathers down there, and you lay those out very carefully inside your nest to keep it warm and cozy, warm and cozy, warm and cozy . . ."

"Don't make me laugh," said Magpie. "I know, I know, I know all that," and off she flew.

Well, not long after that it was time for Magpie to lay her eggs, and she looked out from her perch and saw all of the other birds sitting in their well-built, warm, cozy nests, laying their eggs. "Oh, no," said Magpie, "I don't have anywhere to lay mine! I'd better hurry." And she remembered Sparrow saying something about twigs, and Duck about patting them, and Pigeon saying something about cozy feathers.

So she rushed out and quickly grabbed as many twigs as she could, made a big pile of them, threw a feather on top—and the milk-bottle cap and the earwig and the bus ticket—and she just had time to sit herself down and lay her eggs.

And if you look at a magpie's nest, you'll see that it's always a mess. And she ends up throwing her scrips and scraps and bits and pieces in it too.

I think she likes it like that.

Slowly Does It

Robin Ravilious

Something had invaded the forest—
something strange and worrying.
The Howler Monkey heard it. The
Jaguar smelled it. The Macaws saw
something moving in the bushes.
But no one could tell what it was.

The Something had a strange smell;
it left strange tracks; and it made noises
that the forest had never heard before.
The animals didn't like it at all.

At last the Jaguar—who was bigger

and stronger than the rest—called
a meeting to decide what to do.
Everyone gathered around nervously.
Everyone except the Sloth, that is.
He was asleep, as usual, in his tree.

"Well!" growled the Jaguar in his
deep, fierce voice. "Does anyone
know what this Something is?"

"It's much taller than a monkey," said the Howler Monkey.

"It has a shiny yellow head," said a Macaw.

"It makes a terrible snarling noise," said a Marmoset. "But sometimes it whistles like a bird."

"It smells bad, like fire," said a Snake.

Then the Jaguar asked the question that they were the most worried about. "What does it eat?"

The animals looked at each other in silence. No one knew what it ate. They just hoped that it ate nothing but fruit. The fact was that no one had really seen it at all.

Then the Jaguar had an idea.

"What about that good-for-nothing Sloth?" he growled. "He's been hanging around for weeks. He must have seen it. Go and call the Sloth."

Everyone looked up, and there, high up above them in the tallest tree, was a dirty-looking bundle of hair hanging from a branch. The Howler Monkey went tearing up.

"Hey, you! Slow Boat!" he yelled, shaking the Sloth's branch. "Move yourself. Jaguar wants to have a word with you."

The Sloth was hanging peacefully

by his long,
shaggy arms
and legs,
with his head
resting on his
shaggy chest. Sometimes he ate the
leaves that he could reach. Mostly he
just hung there, fast asleep. He had
hung so still for so long that green
mold was growing in his hair. He
took no notice whatsoever of the
Howler Monkey.

The Howler Monkey shouted and
bounced till fruit rained down on the
animals below, but the Sloth slept on.

Then all of the
little Marmosets
went scampering
up to try waking
him. "Quick, quick,
quick!" they
chattered, jumping
from twig to twig
like grasshoppers.

The Sloth opened his
nearsighted eyes. Then he
closed them again.

The Tree Snake went
next, coiling and
twisting up the tree
and out along
the branch.

"You sshould sstop this ssnoozing," he whispered in the Sloth's ear. "Better ssafe than ssorry."

The Sloth just opened his mouth in a long, slow-motion yawn.

Then the Macaws tried. They flew around and around the Sloth, flashing their bright wings and squawking enough to choke.

"Wake up, you slug. WAKE UP! Jaguar wants to talk."

The Sloth unhooked one arm and scratched his belly drowsily.

Then the Jaguar lost his temper. He leaped and clawed his way up the tree, lashing his tail with rage.

"Look here, you moldy old

hammock," he roared, "are you going to talk, or do I have to make you?"

The Sloth peered at his visitor. "Good . . . morning," he said slowly (although it was afternoon by now). "What . . . seems . . . to . . . be . . . the . . . trouble?"

All of the animals burst out talking at once: growling, yelling, hissing, chattering, and squawking about the Something. The Sloth just hung there smiling and slowly blinking his eyes.

The ruckus went on for some time, for the Sloth wasn't very bright. It took a while to get a new idea into his shaggy head.

"A . . . Something?" he said at last.

"What . . . sort . . . of . . . "

"Stop!" interrupted the
Howler Monkey. "Listen!"
Everyone was quiet. Up from the
ground far beneath them came a
noise more terrifying than anything
that they had ever heard before. An
ugly, earsplitting, snarling roar it was,
and it filled them with fear. Then
there was a loud crack, a huge crash,
and one of the nearby trees just . . .

fell down. The animals could not
believe their eyes.

"The Something," whispered the
Jaguar with his fur
standing on end. "It's
eating the trees."

At that, they all
fled in panic,
tumbling helter-
skelter through
the branches to
get away. In a
moment they
were all gone. All except the Sloth,
of course. He was left hanging there
alone, with his mouth open and his
question unanswered.

"Nobody . . . tells . . . me . . . anything," he said with a sigh. "I . . . s'pose . . . I'd . . . better . . . go . . . and . . . see . . ."

Then, at last, he started to move. Inch by inch he crept along his branch until he reached the main trunk. The awful noise went on and on, but he took no notice. He wrapped his shaggy arms around the tree and began to climb down. Slowly—oh so slowly—he groped his way down and down . . . and down. It was dark under the trees, and the noise had stopped, but still he toiled on. He was almost there, and feeling so tired, when into the clearing came . . . the Something. They stared at each other.

What the Sloth saw was a man. A man with a chain saw to cut down trees. But the Sloth didn't know that it was a man. He'd never met one before. He peered at it doubtfully. Then he did what sloths always do to keep out of trouble: he stayed very still and smiled.

But what the man saw, however, in the shadowy forest, far from home, was a horrible hairy hobgoblin leering at him with a spooky grin on its face. It made his blood run cold. He let out a strangled cry and ran for his life.

The next morning, the other animals came anxiously creeping back. They sniffed the air for that

frightening smell. They listened for the frightening noise. But all they smelled were sweet forest scents; and all they heard were the friendly forest calls. The Something had gone. And there was the Sloth, dangling from his branch in the sunshine, slowly stuffing leaves into his smile.

The Little Elephant's Next Best Thing

Mary Rayner

There was once a little elephant who lived in the hills of south India with his mother and all of his aunties, in the teak forest.

One day, he was splashing around in the river while his mother was being bathed. He squirted water at the other young elephants, and they squealed and squirted back. Then the little elephant looked up and saw a

balloon
floating high
up in the sky. And
underneath the balloon
was a basket, and in the basket,
just looking at the view, was a man.
I would like to do that, thought the
little elephant. *It would be better
than splashing, better than squirting.
It would be the next best thing
to flying.*

He asked his mother how he
could go up in a balloon.

"Don't be silly," said his mother. "You are too small."

So the little elephant waited for the weeks to go by, and then he asked one of his aunties.

"Don't be silly," said the auntie. "You are too heavy."

Oh dear, thought the little elephant. *First I was too small, and now I'm too heavy. I will eat less, and then I will be able to go up in the balloon.*

So he stopped crunching up bamboo leaves, and every time he was hungry he thought about floating through the sky, until the man who cared for the elephants said, "Dear me, this little elephant is

getting too thin. Little elephant,
what is the matter?"

The little elephant said, "I want to
be thin because then I will not be
too heavy to go up in a balloon."

"Ay yai," said the man. "But little
elephant, you are growing up, and
you will soon be too big."

The little elephant
began to cry.

"It is not too late," said the man kindly. "We will get a balloon made. Soon, soon. All we need is money." So he thought and he thought, and then he said, "Little elephant, come with me, and we will go to the town."

They waved goodbye to the little elephant's mother and all of the aunties and set off together for the big town. They walked along the hot, dusty road for miles and miles, past fields of sugar cane and groves of coconut palms and across a dry riverbed.

"I am thirsty," said the tired little elephant.

"Soon, soon, we will be there," said the man.

They came to a stand beside the road, next to a garage. The elephant man asked for a cup of tea and a drink for his elephant. The elephant filled his trunk with water from a bucket, squirted the water into his mouth, and drank it all down. The man fetched some more.

Just then a bus pulled up, full of people. The driver got out and said, "I need more gas, and no one can see out of the windows because they are so dusty."

The little elephant became very excited. "I will squirt the windows clean," he said to his friend.

"Tell all of your passengers to give us some money," said the elephant man, "and my elephant will clean your bus."

So the little elephant squirted water all over the bus, and all of the passengers were pleased and gave

money to the elephant man.

When the bus had left, the garage man said, "That was good. If you would like to stay in the compound behind my stand and garage, you can clean all of the buses that stop here. Everyone likes your elephant."

So the elephant man and the little elephant stayed for many weeks, until they had cleaned a great many buses and saved up a great deal of money.

"Now it is time to go to the town," said the elephant man. They waved goodbye to the garage man and set off again along the hot, dusty road. They went to find the man who made hot-air balloons.

The elephant man explained that the little elephant wanted to ride in a balloon.

The balloon maker shook his head. "That is not possible," he said. "Your elephant is too heavy."

"Can you not make me one especially for him?" asked the elephant man.

"Not possible," said the balloon maker.

"We can pay," said the elephant man, and he tipped out fat

bundles of money in a pile on the ground.

"May be possible after all," said the balloon maker. "Come back in three weeks."

The little elephant and his friend went away, and they waited for three weeks, and then they came back again.

The balloon maker had made a beautiful orange-and-yellow balloon. It lay on the ground behind the store, and tied onto it was an enormous basket—an elephant-size basket with some extra space for the elephant man.

"Now I will tell you how to do

it," said the balloon maker, and he showed them how to fill the balloon with hot air to make it rise up into the sky.

So the balloon was filled with hot air, and just as it lifted off the ground, the little elephant and his

friend scrambled inside the basket.
Up into the sky they went, and
they waved goodbye to the balloon
maker. Slowly, all of the white
houses of the town and even the
big palace became tiny, tinier than
toys. They floated along above the
dusty road, over the dry riverbed,
and over the coconut palms, and
over the sugar-cane fields, until they
came toward the hills.

On their way they saw the garage
and the stand, and they waved, and
the garage man waved back and
cheered and clapped. And they
passed a bus full of tourists, and
they waved, and the bus driver and

all of the tourists waved back and cheered and clapped.

It was just getting to be evening when at last they came to the teak forest. Now they could see the river. They came down a little lower, and the little elephant began to squeal and trumpet because he could see his mother and all of the aunties being bathed.

All of the big, old elephants looked up, and they saw the huge orange-and-yellow balloon, and the little elephant waving his trunk, and his friend beside him.

"Just look at my son!" said his mother, and she put up her trunk and trumpeted to him.

The balloon came down on the
ground, and the little elephant
climbed out. His mother and all of

the aunties welcomed him back, and all of the young elephants had an extra splashy and squirty game with him because he had been away for so long.

The Hedgehog's Race

Duncan Williamson

If you were to travel to the hills of Scotland today, you would find that hedgehogs and hares live together. They're great friends. It wasn't always so . . .

Early every morning, old Mr. Brown Hare came down from his bed in the hillside. He was bound for the farmer's field because his breakfast was turnips. He loved the young turnips coming up and their leaves. But this one morning, bright and early, as old Mr. Hare came hopping down the hillside, the first person he met was old Mr. Hedgehog. And he was crawling around the hedges hunting for his breakfast—snails and slugs and worms, which hedgehogs love to eat! Because Mr. Hare was feeling very frisky this morning, he rubbed his paws together and said to himself, *Oh, ho, old Mr. Hedgehog! I'm going to have some fun this morning!* He liked to tease old Mr. Hedgehog, you know!

So when he came down to the gate leading to the farmer's field, old Mr. Hedgehog of course sat up with his wee pointed nose and his little short legs. And old Mr. Hare said, "Good morning, Short Legs!"

Now, hedgehogs are very sensitive about their short legs. And they don't like it very much when somebody talks about them, because their legs really are very short! He said, "You know, my friend Mr. Hare, you are not a very nice person."

"And why," said old Mr. Hare, "am I not a nice person?"

"Well," he said, "every time we meet, you're always talking about my legs. I can't help it that I have short legs, because I was born like this."

Mr. Hare said, "Wouldn't you like to have long legs like me? You know, I have beautiful legs. I can run faster than anyone! Dogs can't even catch me. Wouldn't it be nice if your legs were like mine and you could run as fast as the wind across the fields?"

And old Mr. Hedgehog said, "Well, of course it would be nice to have long legs like you. But you see, Mr. Hare, you don't need long legs to run fast, you know."

"*You don't need long legs to run fast?*" said old Mr. Hare. "Nonsense! How in the world can you run fast with those short little legs you've got? No way could you run out of the way of a dog or a fox, like me. As for me, I can run swifter than the wind!"

"Well," said old Mr. Hedgehog, "you see, my friend, I'll tell you what I'll do for you. I'll make a bargain with you. I'll challenge you to a race!"

And old Mr. Hare cocked up his ears and said, "Am I hearing right? You mean you're challenging me to a race?"

"Of course!" said old Mr. Hedgehog. "Are you getting deaf in your old age? I said a race!"

Old Mr. Hare said, "You mean you want to race me?"

"Of course," said old Mr. Hedgehog, "I want to race you! I

want to prove to you once and for all that even though I have short legs, I can run faster than you."

"Never!" said old Mr. Hare. "No way can you run faster than me."

"Well," said old Mr. Hedgehog, "would you like to prove it?"

"Of course," said old Mr. Hare, rubbing his paws with glee. "This is going to be fun! I'd love to prove it!"

"Well," said old Mr. Hedgehog, "tomorrow morning I will

meet you here at this gate, and I will race you to the foot of the five-acre field. And I'll race you back again. And I will beat you. Will you promise me one thing?"

"Anything," said old Mr. Hare, "I'll promise you!"

"That you'll never call me Short Legs again as long as you live!"

Old Mr. Hare said, "Look, if you want to race me, I'll race you. And

then I'll beat you like you've never
been beaten in all of your life. And
I'll go so fast that you will never
even see me pass you by. And after I
beat you, I will keep on calling you
Short Legs all the days of your life!"

"Well," said old Mr. Hedgehog,
"we'll just have to wait and see."

"Done!" said old Mr. Hare.
"Tomorrow morning at daybreak
I'm going to teach you a lesson that
you will never forget!"

"Well," said old Mr. Hedgehog,
"we'll just have to wait and see. But
remember now, Mr. Hare, I'll be here."

"Oh," said old Mr. Hare, "I'll
be here!"

And just like that off went Mr.
Hare for his breakfast in the
farmer's turnip field.

But what do you think old Mr.
Hedgehog did? He toddled back to
his little nest where his old wife
lived, old Mrs. Hedgehog! And he
said, "My dear, would you do
something for me?"

Of course, old Mrs. Hedgehog,
she loved her old
husband, Mr.
Hedgehog, very
much. She said,
"Of course,
husband, I'll do
anything for you!"

He said, "You see, my dear, I've challenged Mr. Hare to a race."

She said, "Husband, have you lost your mind? Have you gone crazy?"

"No, my dear, I haven't gone crazy. But," he said, "if you will agree to help me, I will teach old Mr. Hare a lesson that he will never forget."

She said, "What do you want me to do, husband?"

"Well," he said, "it's so simple! You know, old Mr. Hare thinks that he's very smart? But he's not as smart as he thinks he is. Because, like everyone else, he doesn't know you from me." (Neither do I! If you met two hedgehogs, you wouldn't know

a Mr. from a Mrs., would you?)

"Well," she said, "husband, what
do you want me to do?"

He said, "My dear, all I want you
to do is . . . I want you to wait till
daybreak. I will wait up at the top

of the field till Mr. Hare comes
down from the hillside, from his
bush. And I will challenge him to
a race. But I'm not going to run at
all, and neither are you! I want you
to wait at the foot of the field. And
when old Mr. Hare comes down to
the foot of the field, all you have to
do is just stand up and say, 'I'm here
before you!' And I will wait up at
the top of the field, and I won't
move. Silly old Mr. Hare will never
know you from me!" So the plan
was made.

That night, after giving her old
husband, Mr. Hedgehog, a little hug,
off she went. And she wandered

away down to the foot of the field.
There she waited. It was the
summertime, and the nights were
not very long. And of course old
Mr. Hare was very bright in the
morning. He liked to be up early,
at half past four when the sun came
up! So old Mr. Hedgehog, he

crawled away to the gate, and there he waited. He never looked for a worm; he never looked for a snail. He waited for Mr. Hare!

But as soon as the sun began to rise, down came old Mr. Hare, so proud of himself. He was going to show old Mr. Hedgehog this morning how to run—like he'd never run before in all of his life. And then he was going to keep on calling him Short Legs every time they met. See? And many other things. Slow Boat and things like that!

So when Mr. Hare came to the gate, there sat old Mr. Hedgehog.

He said, "Good morning, Short

Legs, are you ready?"

Of course, Mr. Hedgehog, who was very sensitive about his short legs, said, "You promised that you wouldn't call me Short Legs anymore!"

He said, "Of course, I promised you—but after the race! You haven't beaten me yet. And you don't have one single chance in this world. I'm going to beat you, and this morning, because I feel so frisky, I'm going to show you what it's like to run! After I beat you, I'm going to keep on calling you Short Legs all of your life and many other things!"

"Well," said old Mr. Hedgehog, thinking to himself, *She'll be at the bottom of the field by this time.* He was happy. He said, "Okay, Mr. Hare, are you ready?"

And Mr. Hare said, "As ready as

I'll ever be!" He rubbed his paws together and said, "One, two, three—off we go!"

And old Mr. Hare, off he flew down that field faster than he'd ever run. Old Mr. Hedgehog sat there and watched him running like he'd never run before in his life. But he was in for a big surprise. When he came to the foot of the field, there in front of him was old Mrs. Hedgehog.

She said, "I'm here before you!"

And as quick as a wink, old Mr. Hare turned, and he ran back up the field as fast as he could. But on the way up he ran faster! When he came to the top of the field, there was old Mr. Hedgehog.

And old Mr. Hedgehog said, "I'm here before you!"

As quick as a wink, old Mr. Hare turned again, and down that field he ran, faster than he had ever ran before! But when he came to the foot of the field, there was old Mrs. Hedgehog!

She said, "I'm here before you!" And of course poor old Mr. Hare, not knowing Mrs. Hedgehog from Mr. Hedgehog, he turned again! Up the field he flew as fast as he could run.

But then old Mr. Hedgehog said, "I'm still here before you!"

So up and down and up and down ran old Mr. Hare, till at last he was completely exhausted. He

could not run another step. He
came up to the top of the field, and
he was lying there, his tongue
hanging out. And he was panting.

He said, "Tell me, Mr. Hedgehog,
tell me, please! How in the world
did you ever do it?
You ran so fast
that I never
even saw
you pass
me by!"

"Of course," said old Mr. Hedgehog, "I told you! You wouldn't believe me that you don't need long legs to run fast, you know!"

"Well," said old Mr. Hare, "you really beat me there, and I'm still not sure how you did it, but I promise you, my friend, I will never call you Short Legs again as long as I live!"

And that's why today, if you're up in the gorse hills, in the woods, you will find hedgehogs and hares asleep in the same bush—because they are very good friends! And as for old Mr. Hare, he never called Mr.

Hedgehog Short Legs again. But of course you and I know that he beat him by a trick, didn't he? But we're not going to tell Mr. Hare, are we?

How the Lemur Got Her Tail

Mary Hoffman

Long, long ago, before there was
you, before there was me, before
there were any other people in the
world, Lemur lived in Africa. She
was gray all over then, with a long,
bushy gray tail that she held high
up above her back like a flag. The
other animals could always see her
coming as she walked across the
forest floor.

"Good morning, Lemur," called

Chameleon, flicking out his long, sticky tongue. "Where are you off to on this hot, sunny morning?"

"I'm going across the water," said Lemur, "where the baobab trees are shady and the sweet figs grow. Why don't you come too?"

So the Chameleon followed after. He was slower than Lemur, but he didn't get lost because he could always see her bushy tail.

Up in the air flew

Red Kingfisher. "Good morning, Lemur," he sang. "Where are you and Chameleon off to on this hot, sunny morning?"

"We're going across the water," said Lemur, "where the rivers are cool and the flowers shine bright in the dark, green forest. Why don't you come too?"

So the Red Kingfisher went with them. He could fly much faster than they could walk, but he didn't lose them because he

could always see Lemur's bushy tail waving above the grass.

Green Boa Snake was slithering across the forest floor. "Good morning, Lemur," she hissed. "Where are you and Chameleon and Red Kingfisher off to on this hot, sunny morning?"

"We're going across the water," said Lemur, "where the rain is warm and the nights are cool. Why don't you come too?"

So the Green Boa Snake joined them. She could move quickly, even though she had no legs. And if she lost them, she could slink up a tree and watch out for Lemur's bushy tail.

As they passed a tree branch, Tiny Golden Frog croaked, "Good morning, Lemur. Where are you going with Chameleon, Red Kingfisher, and Green Boa Snake on this hot, sunny morning?"

"We're going across the water," said Lemur, "where the mountains are red and the great bamboo grows up to the sky. Why don't you come too?"

So the Tiny Golden Frog joined them, leaping from tree to tree with his long, strong back legs and watching out for the gray flag that was Lemur's tail.

Pansy Butterfly darted back and forth in the warm morning air, fluttering her gorgeous blue wings.

"Good morning, Lemur," she chirped. "Where are you going with Chameleon, Red Kingfisher, Green Boa Snake, and Tiny Golden Frog on this hot, sunny morning?"

"We're going across the water," said Lemur, "where the bees make honey from orchids and the wild ginger grows. Why don't you come too?"

So Pansy Butterfly flitted along

above the other animals, keeping an
eye on Lemur's tail.

Suddenly, all of the animals
noticed that Lemur had stopped.
She had come to the edge of the
water. The others stopped too and
looked at the land across the water
that was so full of good things.

"It's all very well for Red

Kingfisher and Pansy Butterfly," said Chameleon doubtfully, "but how are the rest of us going to get across?

The water looks very wide and deep to me."

"It is," said Lemur, "but look again. There are little islands and ridges under the water all the way across. You'll be there in a leap, skip, and jump."

And to show that she was right, she leaped into the water, waving her bushy gray tail to keep her balance as she hopscotched her way across to the other side. All of the others followed one by one. It was the easiest for Tiny Golden Frog and the hardest for Green Boa Snake, but they all got to the other side in the end.

The warm sun soon dried them out, and Lemur led the way to her favorite places. They all found good things to eat—berries and nuts and nectar. It was noon by then, and everyone was feeling full and hot and sleepy.

Lemur stretched out in the shade of a baobab tree. She was so full of figs that she forgot to keep her tail out of the hot sun. She stayed awake just long enough to curl her paws around her eyes to keep out the glare. Then she fell into a deep sleep.

When everyone woke up, it was late, and the long shadows of evening were falling through the green forest.

"We must go back," croaked Tiny Golden Frog. "Where's Lemur? She must show us the way."

"There she is," said Pansy
Butterfly. "She's still asleep. I'll go
down and wake her up."

And the beautiful blue butterfly

flew down and perched on Lemur's nose. So ticklish were her little feet that Lemur woke up with a sneeze. Pansy Butterfly flew away in alarm.

"What happened to your face, Lemur?" she shrieked. "And, oh, what is the matter with your tail?"

All of the animals crowded around to see what had happened to Lemur in her sleep. The fierce sun had broken through the trees and bleached her face white. Around her eyes, where she had shaded them with her paws, there were two big, black circles. And her long, bushy tail, which had been stretched out on the forest floor, was now striped

black and white—black where the
shade of the branches had protected
some parts from the sun
and white where the
sun's powerful midday
rays had shone down
and bleached it.
Lemur led them

all down to the water so that she could look at her reflection. She turned this way and that and waved her tail around.

"It's not bad, you know, Lemur," hissed Green Boa Snake. "We'll be able to see where you are even better now."

"Yes," said Red Kingfisher, "and now you should lead the others back over the water."

But something else had happened while the animals were asleep. The water was deeper and wider, and all of the little underwater islands and ridges had disappeared. The animals couldn't go back. Red Kingfisher and Pansy Butterfly could have flown over the water, but they decided to stay with their friends.

They are all still living there. After all, the great island across the water from Africa was full of good things. Its name is Madagascar. And Ring-tailed Lemur still runs across the forest floor there, holding up her tail like a flag, for all of her friends and family to see.

Clever Rabbit and King Lion

Amoafi Kwapong

Once upon a time, and a very good time it was, there lived in the rainforest of Ghana many animals, and Lion was their king.

King Lion lived in the best cave on one side of the forest, while the rest of the animals shared the other side. The other animals were not amused, but they had no choice but to remain where they were.

Clever Rabbit was a very close

friend of Madam Hare. Clever Rabbit was very quick at solving problems and riddles, which earned her the title of "Clever." Madam Hare was known in the whole wide forest as a kindhearted lady. With her long ears, Madam Hare could hear a long distance away.

One day, Madam Hare overheard King Lion talking to his wife. He was boasting about a plan to eat up Clever Rabbit. He had already eaten most of the little animals in the forest.

"Today," he said, "it's Clever Rabbit's turn."

Madam Hare was very upset. She

hurried to tell Clever Rabbit what she had heard. At first Clever Rabbit was very upset too. She thought to herself, *I mind my own business, and I don't deserve this.* Madam Hare tried to console her, but Clever Rabbit said, "Action is what I need."

Clever Rabbit thought quickly, and she came up with an idea.

"I'll go to King Lion's cave and offer myself to him. I bet he'll be so confused that he won't eat me just yet."

"Very good," replied Madam Hare.

Clever Rabbit set out for King Lion's cave.

Meanwhile, King Lion was on his way to Clever Rabbit's burrow. Halfway down the path, King Lion and Clever Rabbit met face-to-face. King Lion's eyes were red, and he looked fierce. Clever Rabbit put on a brave face and a smile. She greeted King Lion. "Good morning,

your majesty. I heard you were
going to eat me up for dinner
today. So I wanted to
make it easier for
you by offering
myself to
you."

"Don't be saucy, you little rascal," answered King Lion.

Clever Rabbit continued, "I didn't mean to be saucy, your majesty, but on second thought, I don't think you'll enjoy eating me just yet.

Give me three weeks to fatten up for you. You see, I'm all bones."

"Very well," retorted King Lion. "I can wait three weeks."

So off went Clever Rabbit to her burrow, stopping on the way to tell Madam Hare the good news. "Hurrah! Hurrah!" cried the two friends.

A week passed, but Clever Rabbit looked the same. A second week passed, and still Clever Rabbit had not added an ounce of flesh to her skinny body.

After two weeks, King Lion began to count the seconds, the minutes, and the hours. Day one came and went. Then it was day two, day three, day four, day five, day six, and day seven!

"Three weeks are up! I'm going to feast on rabbit today!" gloated King Lion.

Clever Rabbit dressed in her prettiest clothes, with bows in her hair. On her way to King Lion's cave, she stopped to chat to Madam Hare. Madam Hare wished Clever Rabbit the best of luck, saying, "I trust that you'll come back again."

"Thank you," said Clever Rabbit, "I certainly need a lot of luck today." And off she went.

When she arrived at King Lion's cave, King Lion was working up his appetite. He was just about to pounce on Clever Rabbit when she said, "Oh, your majesty, you should hear this! There's a bigger lion not too far away from here who's been competing with you. He's eating all of the little animals there, and I hear that he's eaten more than you have."

"Is that so?" said King Lion.

"Show me the way to this arrogant

lion, and I'll soon fix him."

Clever Rabbit led the way. She was so overjoyed at not being gobbled up by King Lion that she began to sing, dance, and skip along the path. King Lion was not amused. He roared at Clever Rabbit, "Stop singing, dancing, and skipping at once!" Clever Rabbit stopped at once.

Soon they were both standing by a lake. Clever Rabbit pointed to a spot where King Lion should stand and look in the water. King Lion quickly stood on that spot and stretched to look in the water. There was another lion! As quick as a flash, King Lion jumped into the